SABAN'S POWER RANGERS
NINJA STEEL

NINJA
STEEL
MAGIC

by Sara Schonfeld

Penguin Young Readers Licenses
An Imprint of Penguin Random House

PENGUIN YOUNG READERS LICENSES
An Imprint of Penguin Random House LLC

ISBN 9780515159882   10 9 8 7 6 5 4 3 2 1

The Ninja Power Stars are in danger of falling into the wrong hands! Evil warrior Galvanax wants to use them to control the galaxy. A new generation of warriors must rise up to protect the Ninja Power Stars—they are the Power Rangers! When they aren't saving the world, they're normal teenagers at Summer Cove High School. Their names are Brody, Calvin, Hayley, Sarah, and Preston.

One morning before school, Preston made an announcement.

"Ladies and gentlemen!" he said. "Time for a moment of amazement from master magician Presto Change-O!"

His friends and fellow Power Rangers Brody, Calvin, Hayley, and Sarah cheered him on.

"Let's hope this one works," Sarah said quietly.

But two students, Victor Vincent and Monty, were watching the show, too.

"More like Presto Lame-O," Victor said. Then he ran over to Preston. "Let me see that hat."

And before Preston could stop him, Victor reached into the hat and pulled out a rabbit!

As the other kids saw the trick revealed, they started to boo. Preston's magic show was over, and it was another failure.

Meanwhile, the Warrior Dome spaceship orbited Earth. Inside, Galvanax was looking for the next monster that could destroy the Power Rangers and bring him the Ninja Power Stars and the Ninja Steel. But no monster seemed powerful enough!

"It's time the Power Rangers faced a true heavyweight," said Ripcon to his master. "Like you!"

Galvanax roared with approval.

"I'll start by destroying that Red Ranger twerp who stole my Ninja Nexus Prism!" he said. "That will prove once again that there's only one true *Galaxy Warriors* Champion!"

Brody met Preston at his locker.

"Don't worry, Presto," Brody said. "Just keep practicing."

"When I was five, my parents took me to a magic show," Preston said. "The magician made this dragon bracelet appear on my wrist! Ever since then, I've always wanted to be a magician."

"I've trained to be a ninja since I could walk, and it was a struggle," Brody said. "One day, it just started to click."

Suddenly they both heard a scratching noise in Preston's hat.
Preston reached in and pulled out a rabbit.
"See!" Brody said. "That trick was flawless."
"You don't understand," Preston said. "This isn't my rabbit. I only have one!"
He put the hat back on his head, and they heard the noise again!
He pulled out a third rabbit.
"I guess magic must be starting to click with me!" Preston said.

Preston went to shop class to talk to Mick and his team, in case his new magic had to do with the Ninja Steel.

Calvin and Hayley were fixing Brody's dad's old car. Hayley rested her drink on the hood. When she slammed the car door, her drink went flying.

Preston yelled, pointing a wrench at the drink. It froze in midair! The other kids looked at Preston in amazement. "I stopped the drink!" Preston said. "I can do real magic!"

"I seriously doubt that," Calvin said.

"Really?" Preston said. He yelled, "Release!" The drink fell right on Calvin's face.

"Did these powers start recently?" Mick asked. As Preston explained, Mick gasped. "It's the Ninja Steel!" he said. "Legend has it that the Ninja Steel can magnify your truest desires. Preston, you need to be very careful using this new power."

Meanwhile, Sarah's Ninjacom pinged with a message from Brody. Buzzcams were nearby, which meant that a new monster would soon appear to fight them.

Brody saw people running away, so he ran right toward the monster.

And it wasn't just any monster. It was Galvanax and his evil henchmen!

"Ten years ago, you destroyed my father and imprisoned me on your ship. But now, this Ninja Power Star is going to help me destroy you!" Brody said.

"You fool, you don't stand a chance against me!" Galvanax roared.

"Well, I won't be fighting you," Brody said. "*We* will!" And the other Power Rangers appeared!

Even though the Power Rangers were scared, they didn't want Galvanax to know! Sarah and Hayley started to tease him.

But Madame Odius, Galvanax's spy, was smart. She knew that Galvanax couldn't defeat five Power Rangers.

"You're out of practice. If they knock you down once, you will look weak," she said.

Galvanax knew she was right.

Galvanax pointed at Brody.

"You're the traitor I'm after. You're the one who stole from me," he said. "When you're ready to fight me, we can settle this. But for now, meet Slogre!"

With that, Galvanax disappeared, and a horrible monster that looked like a turtle appeared in his place!

The Power Rangers prepared to fight. They locked in and activated their Ninja Power Stars and morphed into Power Rangers!

Calvin, Hayley, Preston, and Sarah fought the Kudabots, Galvanax's henchmen. Then they helped Brody fight Slogre.

"When you pick on one of us," Sarah said, "you pick on all of us!"

Slogre used his thick shell to defend himself from the Power Rangers' attack, and then shot a strange liquid into their faces.

Brody, Calvin, Hayley, and Sarah fell over.

"Time for a little magic," Preston said. He conjured a dragon, and its fire breath sent Slogre into the river!

Brody went to help the other Power Rangers get up.

"Wasn't that dragon I made awesome?" Preston bragged.

"It was pretty cool," Sarah said. "I mean . . . hot."

"You know," Preston said, "I think I'm ready to show the world some real magic!"

But the Power Rangers didn't know that Slogre wasn't destroyed—and that his turtle poison would soon start to work!

Back at school, Preston made another announcement.

"Ladies and gentlemen," he said. "Prepare yourself for some fantastic magic. But first, I need a volunteer."

And he called Victor Vincent up to the stage.

The Rangers wanted to watch, but Slogre's poison made them feel tired. They decided to go home to rest.

As Calvin, Hayley, and Sarah left, Preston waved his wand over the hat.

"Herble-derble, woolen mitten, let Victor find a gentle kitten!"

Victor reached in and pulled out a gigantic roaring puma!

For his next trick, Preston tried to saw Monty in half . . . but then Monty's legs ran away!

"We can fix this later," Brody said, running over. "I just got a message from Hayley. Something's wrong!"

Brody and Preston ran outside. Their friends were moving like they were in slow motion, and Slogre was back!

When Calvin, Hayley, and Sarah tried to morph, Slogre grabbed their Ninja Power Stars right out of their hands!

There was nothing they could do but watch the monster run away with their stars!

When Slogre saw Brody and Preston, he wasn't scared.

"Fantastic!" he said. "More Power Rangers! Hand over your Power Stars, now!"

Brody knew the two of them couldn't defeat Slogre alone.

"Use your magic," he said to Preston.

"It's not working right!" Preston said. "You saw what happened with Monty."

"Just try," Brody said.

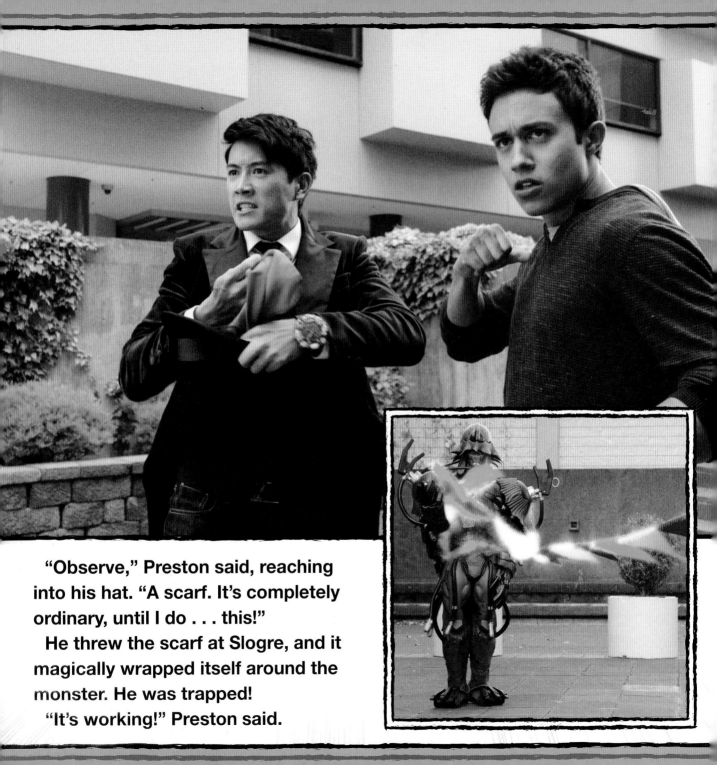

"Observe," Preston said, reaching into his hat. "A scarf. It's completely ordinary, until I do . . . this!"

He threw the scarf at Slogre, and it magically wrapped itself around the monster. He was trapped!

"It's working!" Preston said.

Brody grabbed the Power Stars from Slogre and returned them to their rightful owners.

"Maybe your magic isn't broken," Brody said. "Maybe you were just using it for the wrong reasons with Victor and Monty."

Preston thought for a second.

"You think my magic only works when I'm—"

"—helping others," Brody finished.

But Preston's magic was wearing off, and Slogre freed himself!

Preston and Brody morphed into Power Rangers and used their Ninja Star Blades to attack Slogre.

"Red and Blue Ninja Spirit Steel Slash, Ninja Spin!" they yelled together. "Final Attack!"

He was finally defeated! Destroying Slogre healed Calvin, Hayley, and Sarah. They were moving at normal speed again.

Back in the Warrior Dome above Earth, the cheering monster crowd voted to give Slogre another chance. He returned gigantified—bigger and scarier than ever!

The Power Rangers called their Megazord to take him down.

Slogre could fly! As he jumped, he shot more poisonous mist at the Megazord.

"He's not the only one who can fly," Preston said. "Let's try Dragon Formation! Combine!"

The Megazord morphed into Dragon Formation, and now it had wings!

They found Slogre above the clouds. The Megazord hit Slogre with its tail, and then with its powerful dragon breath!

The Power Rangers yelled out together, "Dragon Lightning, Final Attack!"

"Show's over," Brody announced. "Ninjas win!"

Back at school, Mick helped Preston put Monty back together.

"Two half Montys, here and there," Preston chanted. "Combine them into one, fair and square!"

Monty stood up. His body was back together, but it was square!

Luckily, Monty liked it. He ran away to enjoy some square dancing, eat three square meals—and maybe try boxing before the magic wore off!

"I'm sorry for showing off my magic when I really should have been helping you. Guess I got a little carried away," Preston said.

"It's okay," Hayley said. "We forgive you."

"And there's one more surprise," Calvin said. They blindfolded Brody and led him to the garage.

Calvin removed the blindfold.

"No way! My dad's old car! You fixed it!" Brody said. "This is so epic!"

"Now, everywhere you go, you'll have a little bit of your dad with you," Hayley said.

"I love you guys," Brody said. "This is the best gift ever. Thank you so much!"

All the Power Rangers piled into the car, and they drove off in search of their next adventure!